Author's Note

The Tale of Rabbit and Coyote, from the town of Juchitán, in Oaxaca, Mexico, weaves together several traditional threads of story: tales of Brer Rabbit, the story of Coyote swallowing the moon, and the origin of "the rabbit in the moon." (In Mexico the legend says it's a rabbit who lives there, not a man!) The version of this tale that I read was written in Spanish by the painter Francisco Toledo. I was drawn to it by the zest of the language and the echoes of Uncle Remus; American readers will certainly recognize the trickster rabbit and his exploits. To that audience—and to those who have never met Rabbit and Coyote before—I am glad to present these characters in a particularly Mexican form.

THE TALE OF RABBIT AND COYOTE

by **Tony Johnston**

illustrated by **Tomie dePaola**

G. P. Putnam's Sons
New York

... • FOR MY ADORADA CHAR
— FOREVER IN THE MIDST OF CHIRIPIORCAS.
—TJ

... AND FOR MY FOLK-ART FRIEND
— ALICE ANN BIGGERSTAFF.
—TdeP

G. P. Putnam's Sons, a division of The Putnam & Grosset Group, 200 Madison Avenue,
New York, NY 10016. G. P. Putnam's Sons, Reg. U.S. Pat. & Tm. Off.
Published simultaneously in Canada. Printed in Hong Kong by South China Printing Co. (1988) Ltd.
Type designed by Patrick Collins. Text set in Meridien Medium

Library of Congress Cataloging-in-Publication Data
Johnston, Tony.   The tale of Rabbit and Coyote / by Tony Johnston;
illustrated by Tomie dePaola.   p.   cm.
Summary: Rabbit outwits Coyote in this Zapotec tale which explains why coyotes howl at the moon.
1. Zapotec Indians—Legends. 2. Rabbit (Legendary character) 3. Coyote (Legendary character)
[1. Coyote (Legendary character) 2. Zapotec Indians—Legends. 3. Indians of Mexico—Legends.
4. Animals—Folklore.] I. dePaola, Tomie, ill. II. Title.
F1221.Z3J65   1994   398.2′089976—dc20   92-43652 CIP AC   ISBN 0-399-22258-8

1 3 5 7 9 10 8 6 4 2

First Impression

One full-moon night, Rabbit found a field of *chiles.*
He was so pleased to see them, all glossy and green,
that he jumped right in and ate the biggest ones.

When the sun rose, the farmer came to check the *chiles*. They were scattered everywhere. And the biggest, glossiest, greenest ones were GONE!

Among the plants he saw rabbit tracks. So what did he do?
He made himself a beeswax doll. And he set that doll in
the middle of the field to catch the *chile* thief.

When night fell, Rabbit returned. He saw the farmer
made of wax and crept up to say hello (and to ask for some
chiles too).

But the wax farmer had nothing to say to Rabbit. Nothing
at all.

Rabbit was angry.

¡QUÉ PERSONA TAN PEGAJOSA!

He punched the farmer. Hard. His right paw stuck in the wax. Still, the farmer said nothing. So he punched him once again. His left paw stuck too.

Rabbit was fuming mad. But the wax farmer was silent as the stars. So he hauled off with both feet and walloped him. *Ay, ay, ay!* Then Rabbit was trapped for sure!

When the real farmer came to check his trap, he was delighted to see Rabbit there.

"*Qué delicioso.* How delicious," he said, rubbing his hands together. He popped Rabbit into a sack and took him home.

When he got there, he hung up the sack, built a fine
fire and set a pot of water to boil. Then he went looking
for herbs.

From where he was hanging in the sack, Rabbit saw
Coyote coming.

"What are you doing there?" asked Coyote.

"This man wants me to marry his daughter," Rabbit said, "but I'm too young. Why don't you take my place? Look, the water's ready to make hot chocolate. There will be a grand party."

When the farmer came back and took down the sack, he saw Coyote inside it.

"You'll pay for this," he said.

He popped Coyote into the hot water. *Ay, ay, ay!* Coyote flew right out of that water and took off after Rabbit.

He followed his tracks till he found him high in a *jícara* tree.

"I'm going to eat you now," said Coyote. For he was very furious.

So what did Rabbit do?

Well, he knew that Coyote couldn't tell the difference between the fruit of the *jícara,* hard as a rock, and the soft, sweet *zapote.*

"Why eat me," asked Rabbit, "when right here I have sweet *zapote* fruit instead?"

"Well, toss me one," growled Coyote.

Rabbit did that. He tossed down the *jicara* with all his might. *Plonk!* It struck Coyote and knocked him out cold as a cabbage.

When Coyote woke up, he tracked Rabbit till he saw that furry scoundrel resting against a large rock at the edge of a hill.

"Please, don't eat me," pleaded Rabbit, leaning against the rock. "Can't you see that if I don't hold back this rock it will roll down and crush the world? Here, you hold it while I find some people to help us."

Coyote believed Rabbit and took his place. Rabbit hopped
off free as a bee.

Soon, Coyote knew he'd made a mistake. He went after Rabbit, muttering all the while.

When at last he found him, Coyote said, "*Now* I'll eat you!"

"But then who will take care of the little children in this little school?" asked Rabbit, pointing to a wasps' nest on a low tree branch. "Someone needs to give it a knock if a pupil tries to leave."

Well, Coyote loved to give knocks. So he took the job.
He lay near the branch and waited. When a wasp flew out,
he whacked that wasp nest with a little stick. And—all
the wasps came after him! They chased him into a pond.
Only his nose stuck out of the water. So they stung that
many times.

It was pitch-black night when Coyote found Rabbit at the edge of a lake. Now he was *really* going to eat him.

But Rabbit said, "Why eat me, Coyote, when I have been waiting for you so we can share the cheese that you see there?"

Rabbit pointed to the moon's reflection upon the water.

"Of course," explained Rabbit, "we must first drink all the juice of the cheese in order to eat the cheese itself."

So Coyote began drinking the water to reach the cheese itself.

After a time he said, "I simply can't drink more."

"Just a few more sips," said Rabbit, "and you'll reach the cheese for sure."

Coyote drank more, more, MORE. He drank so much that
water poured from his ears. But when he turned to discuss
this with Rabbit, Rabbit ran away.

Coyote ran after him as best he could, but he was swollen as a sponge.

Now Rabbit knew of a ladder that reached into the sky. He began to climb it. Up, up, up. And he hopped all the way to the moon.

Then he hid the ladder.

Far below, he saw Coyote looking for him up in the sky.

But try as he might, Coyote never found the ladder.

That is why, to this very day,
Coyote sits gazing at the moon.

And now and then he howls at it.
For he is still *very* furious with Rabbit.

Glossary of Spanish Expressions

Hola, cena.	OH-la, SAY-nah*	Hello, dinner.
¡Mis chiles!	meess CHEE-layss	My chili peppers!
¡Conejo malvado!	koh-NAY-ho mahl-VAH-doh	Wicked rabbit!
¡Qué persona tan pegajosa!	kay pehr-SOH-nah tahn pay-gah-HO-sah	What a sticky person!
Te voy a comer, manito.	tay voy ah koh-MEHR, mah-NEE-toh	I'm going to eat you, little buddy!
¡Hasta luego!	AH-stah loo-AY-goh	See you later!
¡Más, más, más!	mahss, mahss, mahss	More, more, more!
Me siento un poco raro.	May see-EHN-toh oon POH-koh RAH-roh	I feel a bit strange.
¡Adiós, amigo!	ah-dee-OHSS, ah-MEE-goh	Good-bye, friend!

*These transliterations have been provided to help readers who don't speak Spanish to pronounce the Spanish words. But the best way to learn how to say the words correctly is to ask someone who speaks Spanish fluently to pronounce them for you.